FEMALE FIGURE
SKATING LEGENDS

NANCY KERRIGAN

Paula Edelson

CHELSEA HOUSE PUBLISHERS
Philadelphia

Produced by Choptank Syndicate, Inc.

Editor and Picture Researcher: Norman L. Macht
Production Coordinator and Editorial Assistant: Mary E. Hull
Design and Production: Lisa Hochstein

CHELSEA HOUSE PUBLISHERS

Editor in Chief: Stephen Reginald
Managing Editor: James Gallagher
Production Manager: Pamela Loos
Art Director: Sara Davis
Director of Photography: Judy L. Hasday
Senior Production Editor: Lisa Chippendale
Publishing Coordinator: James McAvoy
Cover Illustration: Keith Trego

Cover Photos: AP/Wide World Photos

The Chelsea House World Wide Web site address is
http://www.chelseahouse.com

First Printing

1 3 5 7 9 8 6 4 2

Library of Congress Cataloging-in-Publication Data

Edelson, Paula.
    Nancy Kerrigan / Paula Edelson.
      p.   cm. — (Female figure skating legends)
    Summary: Discusses the skating career of Nancy Kerrigan, who overcame an attack
  that injured her knee and went on to win a silver medal at the 1994 Olympics.
    Includes bibliographical references (p.   ) and index.
    ISBN 0-7910-5028-9 (hardcover)
    1. Kerrigan, Nancy, 1969–   —Juvenile literature. 2. Skaters—
  United States—Biography—Juvenile literature. [1. Kerrigan, Nancy, 1969–   .
  2. Ice skaters. 3. Women—Biography.] I. Title. II. Series.
  GV850.K38E34   1998
  796.91'2'092—dc21   98-29475
    [b]   CIP
                                                        AC

CONTENTS

A SURPRISE MEDAL WINNER

The American figure skating team that went to Albertville, France, for the 1992 winter Olympics was a very strong one. The three women on the team were Kristi Yamaguchi, the reigning World and United States national champion; Nancy Kerrigan, who finished second to Yamaguchi at the 1992 Nationals and third at the 1991 World Championships; and Tonya Harding, the gold medal winner of the 1991 Nationals.

Nancy was very excited to be skating for her country in her first Olympic competition. She felt very comfortable in Albertville for several reasons. In the first place, she was skating better than she ever had before. Nancy had recently risen from obscurity to win the bronze at the 1991 Nationals and the bronze

Nancy Kerrigan performs during the freestyle portion of competition at the 1992 Olympics in Albertville, France.

at the 1991 World Championships. With her first medal in a major international competition, Nancy felt confident. Yet all the attention was focused on her teammate Kristi Yamaguchi, who was the favorite to win the gold medal. Yamaguchi's chief rivals were expected to be Japan's Midori Ito and Surya Bonaly of France. No one really thought Kerrigan had much of a chance to win a medal, so she felt no pressure.

Nancy was also thrilled that her friend and training partner Paul Wylie had made the men's team. Wylie, the team captain, was a friend of Kerrigan and her family back in Massachusetts.

For seven years Wylie had trained with Evy and Mary Scotvold, a husband-and-wife team of coach and choreographer, at their facility on Cape Cod. The Scotvolds were also Nancy's longtime coaches, and she and Wylie had a lot of fun training together. Nancy's parents, Dan and Brenda Kerrigan, had accompanied their daughter to France, and would be in the arena rooting for her while she skated.

Nancy Kerrigan and Kristi Yamaguchi were roommates in Albertville and close friends. They trained together and ate together, which helped both skaters relax and focus on the competition.

At the 1992 Olympics there was a lot of talk about the talents of Midori Ito, who was going to try to become the first woman to land a triple Axel in Olympic competition. This hardest of all jumps, involving three and a half mid-air rotations and a lot of strength, had been landed for the first time in 1978. Though male skaters sometimes landed triple Axels in competition, few women could successfully perform this demanding jump. The only other woman competing in the 1992 Olympics who had landed the triple Axel in any competition was the American skater Tonya Harding. Harding's athleticism had helped her win some competitions, including the 1991 National Championships, but she was not quite as graceful on the ice as Kerrigan or Yamaguchi. Even so, Harding had planned to include the triple Axel in her short and long program, as had Ito.

For Midori Ito, the Albertville Olympics were the last part of a very long and difficult journey. She had left her home in Tokyo to train in a very small town in Japan, and at the age of 16 had competed in the 1988 Olympics in Calgary. Even though she skated well in the competition, she had just missed a medal, placing fourth. The four years between Calgary and Albertville were marked by constant practices for Ito, who was a very strong and elegant skater. Although Yamaguchi was the more beautiful skater, Ito was very athletic. Observers thought

The 1992 U.S. Women's Olympic Figure Skating team, (from left) Tonya Harding, Nancy Kerrigan, and Kristi Yamaguchi, pose together after their selection for the team.

that if Ito could land her triple Axel in the short and long programs, she had a good chance to win the gold.

Nancy spent the first week of the Olympics watching her teammates compete in the ice skating events. She cheered her friend Paul Wylie, who skated brilliantly. Wylie, who was not favored to place even close to the top in the men's event, skated a wonderful long program and won the silver medal. Wylie's performance excited Nancy, and it also encouraged her. If Paul could win a medal maybe she could too.

The ladies' figure skating program did not begin until the last week of the Olympics. Every day the women practiced in the rink, getting used to the ice and staying in shape. Ito, Yamaguchi, Kerrigan, and France's Surya Bonaly all looked impressive in practice. The competition was still anyone's game.

Then, on the night of the ladies' short program, a very unusual thing happened. Ito was on the ice, warming up along with several other women, including Bonaly. Ito was concentrating very hard on her own skating, and wasn't really watching the others on the ice. Bonaly, on the other hand, was trying to get pumped up for her routine, and she was trying to get the crowd in the stands excited too. Suddenly Bonaly jumped in the air and turned a back flip, landing on one skate. It was a very daring move—one that is not allowed in competition. When Bonaly landed she came so close to Midori Ito that Ito fell to the ice in surprise and shock. Ito's concentration was destroyed for the moment, and it would make a difference during her short program.

Yamaguchi skated a solid and beautiful short program. She landed all of her jumps, including a triple Lutz and double toe loop combination, and had a real presence and beauty to her routine. Bonaly skated next. Although strong and athletic, Bonaly did not have Yamaguchi's grace. But she was French, skating in front of the home crowd, and the audience cheered loudly whenever Bonaly landed a jump. Soon after Bonaly finished, Ito skated onto the ice and began her routine. But it was clear from the beginning that she was not focusing or concentrating well. She looked unsteady, and was not skating cleanly, which was something that she needed to do if she hoped to land her triple Axel. Unfortunately for Ito, she fell dramatically while attempting that jump.

Ito's scores were much lower than they would have been had she skated well, and she was very disappointed as she headed back to the locker room. In the meantime, Nancy Kerrigan was getting ready to skate. The short program was always a strong part of her competition, and if she could skate this one cleanly, she might have a chance at a medal, particularly since Ito had fallen.

Nancy's routine, which she skated to an original composition by Mark Militano, was very clean and crisp. She landed all of her jumps and looked very elegant on the ice. The only skater who scored higher than Nancy that night was her teammate Yamaguchi, who finished the short program in first place.

One of the most memorable parts of Nancy Kerrigan's performance in the short program at Albertville was her mother's reaction to Nancy's skating. Legally blind in one eye and capable of only severely limited vision in the other, Brenda Kerrigan was unable to watch her daughter skate, because she couldn't see well enough. Instead, Brenda sat in a special area of the rink

Japan's Midori Ito, known for her powerful triple Axel, was a favorite to win the 1992 Olympics. Though she fell attempting the difficult jump in her short program, Ito later landed the triple Axel in a flawless long program that secured her the silver medal.

in front of a television monitor, where she could see her daughter skate by putting her face very close to the monitor and watching very carefully. What she saw made her very happy. At the end of the routine Brenda looked up and joyously signaled to her happy daughter. It was a wonderful night for the Kerrigans.

Two days later, on February 21, 1992, the long program took place. Nancy was very nervous; at four minutes the long program is almost twice as long as the short. Skating for four minutes is tiring. Unlike the short program, which lasts under three minutes and includes a required number of moves and jumps, the long program is freestyle. Skaters can showcase their favorite maneuvers, but their scores reflect the difficulty of the moves they choose. Many skaters who have skated a terrific short program at the Olympics have fallen in the long program from sheer exhaustion. In 1988, for example, an American named Debbi Thomas vied with East German skater Katarina Witt for the gold medal. Thomas skated a wonderful short program and was solidly in first place heading for the long program. Then Thomas fell several times during the long program. Although Thomas ended up winning a bronze medal, many people thought that if she had skated the long program as well as she had the short program, she would have won the gold.

These thoughts were probably also on the mind of Kerrigan's teammate Kristi Yamaguchi. She had also competed in Calgary, and remembered Thomas's disastrous performance there. Yamaguchi bore the pressure of being favored to win the first gold medal by an American woman since Dorothy Hamill had triumphed in 1976. In fact, Hamill had even emerged from the crowd to hug Yamaguchi before her performance to wish her luck.

Skating first, Yamaguchi landed her jumps—including five triples—perfectly and skated with a grace that only a few ice skaters are capable of achieving. Her scores reflected the beauty of her program, assuring her of the gold medal. The battle that remained would be for second place.

Then it was Kerrigan's turn. She nervously skated onto the ice in her elegant white costume and began her program. She landed her jumps and looked elegant and gracious, but her nervousness affected her technical merit. She looked a little wobbly and uncertain on the ice, and seemed much stiffer and less at ease than she had two nights earlier at the short program. So Nancy Kerrigan decided to cut two triple jumps to singles and she did not fall. Kerrigan completed her program with a big smile of relief. She was very happy to get through her program without falling, even if it meant changing to easier jumps.

Surya Bonaly was in third place after the short program. Her long program, however, was severely flawed. Although Bonaly did not fall, she missed three of her triples and did not land her jumps with the authority or grace that Yamaguchi had shown. Even so, Bonaly's program was very difficult technically, and the home crowd once again cheered her every move. But the judges marked Bonaly down for what they thought was her lack of artistic flair.

Midori Ito entered the long program in fourth place. She knew she would have to skate her best to place in the top three. That would mean landing the triple Axel. Unlike the short program, though, Ito's long program was superb. Not only did she land the triple Axel, but her other jumps were flawless and clean as well. When the ice had cleared, Ito was in second place.

Although Nancy had not skated her best in the long program, she still had reason to celebrate. She had surprised a field of very strong skaters by outperforming Bonaly to win the bronze medal. At the closing ceremony of the 1992 winter Olympics, Kerrigan was radiant as she performed without pressure in her bright yellow dress. She and fellow American medalist Paul Wylie also skated a number together to the song "The Last Night in the World" from the musical *Miss Saigon*. Nancy was excited about her future. She knew that in two years she would be skating again at the next Olympics in Lillehammer. With Yamaguchi talking about retiring, next time Nancy would be in a good position to win a gold medal.

LONGING TO SKATE

Nancy Kerrigan was born February 7, 1968, in Stoneham, Massachusetts, a small suburban town about 30 miles north of Boston. Nancy was the third and youngest child of Dan and Brenda Kerrigan. Her two older brothers, Mark and Michael, were seven and five when Nancy was born.

When Nancy was about one year old her mother was stricken with a rare eye disease that left her legally blind. Although barely able to see, Brenda did manage to take care of her three children during the long hours her husband Dan spent at his job as a welder. Nancy also spent a lot of time taking care of her mother, sometimes choosing her clothes for her. When she was old enough, Nancy also learned how to put her mother's makeup on for her.

By the time she graduated from Stoneham High School, Nancy Kerrigan had already performed in several major skating competitions.

Dick Button, shown here in a sit spin, was the first skater to complete a triple jump in competition when he landed a triple loop at the 1952 winter Olympics.

Life wasn't always easy for the Kerrigans, but they managed to make the most of their situation. The Kerrigan house was always full of people, warmth, and laughter. They had many friends in the neighborhood. On most days, it seemed, people would come by to say hello and end up staying for dinner. Nancy's grandmother lived just two houses away from the Kerrigans. Because her mother could not see well enough to drive, Nancy and her brothers often relied on their grandmother, or friends and neighbors, to take them places when a car was required. But at home, Brenda Kerrigan was in charge, and was a very loving parent. From her earliest days, Nancy had a friend and a very important fan in her mother.

The Kerrigans lived near the Stoneham ice skating rink. When Nancy was very young, she dreamed about skating there. Nancy had first learned to skate while playing ice hockey with her older brothers, Mark and Michael, but she longed to try figure skating. Then, when she was six years old, she got her wish. The Kerrigans enrolled Nancy in a one-hour skating class for children. The class met once a week at the skating rink. From the moment young Nancy put on her ice skates, it was clear that she was going to be a special skater. Her skating teacher sensed Nancy's talent right away, and told the Kerrigans that it might be a good idea to invest in private skating lessons for their youngest child, who seemed to have so much promise and talent.

Nancy's family was excited to hear this news, but they also knew that it wouldn't be easy to get Nancy the training she needed. Private skating lessons, ice time, and skating equipment are very expensive, and Dan Kerrigan did not make a lot of money as a welder. In addition, Nancy was not their only child.

Dan Kerrigan felt strongly that Nancy should have the training she needed to be a world class ice skater. He knew that his young daughter was happiest when she was skating. Nancy was a very quiet little girl, but once she was on the ice, her shyness seemed to disappear. Her blue eyes lit up with excitement and her brown hair swirled around her. "We'll take things one step at a time," he told his family. Kerrigan hired a coach to give Nancy the skating lessons she wanted. To pay for Nancy's training and make ends meet, Dan Kerrigan worked extra jobs, but he took pains to spend time with his family as well. Every night he returned home to have dinner with his family before going on to his night job.

When Nancy was eight years old, she entered her first skating competition. It would be the first of dozens of tournaments Nancy would skate in during her early years. Her closely-knit family always traveled with her and cheered her on whenever she was on the ice.

As the years went by, they had more and more to cheer. Nancy was skating better and better, and she began winning most of the competitions she entered.

By the time Nancy was ten years old and in the fifth grade, she was skating for four hours every day. Since Nancy, like all other fifth graders, went to school all day Monday through Friday, finding four extra hours each day to practice was not always easy. It meant waking up very early in the morning and skating before other people were even awake. It also meant leaving school and going directly to the rink to train until dinner. To compensate for getting up so early in the morning, Nancy went to bed before most other kids did.

Sometimes Nancy would get up as early as 4:30 in the morning to go to the practice rink before school started. Her mother, Brenda, never forced her to go. In fact, sometimes it was Nancy who did the forcing. "I'd wake her up at 4:30 to skate," Brenda remembered, "and at first she'd say, 'I don't want to go,' and I'd say, 'Okay, don't go,' and she'd say 'but I have to go.'" Every single morning, Nancy would get up, grab her skates, and go to the rink to practice her figures, jumps, footwork, and spins.

As Nancy grew up, she began to compete in tournaments all over the country. This meant a lot of traveling and sacrifices for the Kerrigan family, who always went with her. Dan, Brenda, Michael, and Mark spent many weekends and almost every vacation on the road with Nancy as she competed in USFSA tournaments. Traveling that often was expensive. In addition, Nancy required several new pairs of skates a year, as well as several outfits to wear during competitions. Then there was the training itself, which was always very costly. To pay for all the expenses Dan worked almost around the clock at several jobs.

Because Nancy spent so much time skating, she didn't have as many friends as some of her other classmates at Stoneham Elementary School. It wasn't because Nancy didn't like the other kids in her class. She just didn't have the time to spend socializing that most other children have. Not many girls her age would choose to give up so much in order to ice skate. Her parents told Nancy that if she ever wanted to give up skating, she should. They would never push her to do something she didn't want to do. But Nancy couldn't imagine living any other way. "I just wanted to skate," Nancy said later about her determined childhood.

Nancy's experience as an aspiring skater was not unique. At the same time that she was

Canada's Vern Taylor became the first person to land a triple Axel when he successfully completed three and a half mid-air rotations during the 1978 Worlds in Ottawa. The triple Axel has also been landed by women skaters Midori Ito and Tonya Harding.

getting up at 4:30 in the morning and spending long hours in practice instead of with friends, another American girl who dreamed of becoming an Olympic athlete, Kristi Yamaguchi, was making similar sacrifices. Since there was not enough time for her to squeeze in all her skating practice after school, Kristi, like Nancy, got up around four o'clock in the morning to put in her ice time. In the evenings, while other children were watching television or playing, Kristi would be fast asleep. Though her practice paid off and Kristi became the world's best junior skater by age 16, she felt isolated and regretted the fact that she had never had a normal social life.

Having to put skating in front of everything else in order to succeed was not just an American phenomenon. In countries around the world, girls and young women who aspired to be great skaters were making the same sacrifices of leisure time and friends. Katarina Witt, the East German skater who dominated figure skating in the 1980s, admitted that skating practice was her childhood. She spent more time with her coach than with her family. Though she wanted to have a boyfriend as a teenager, her rigorous schedule made it impossible for her to carry on a relationship. In order to become a star athlete, the Ukrainian skater Oksana Baiul had to leave her home and friends and live with a new family while she trained. Eventually, she even had to leave her homeland, where it had become impossible to find the professional and medical resources necessary for skating.

For every skater whose hard work and personal sacrifices have succeeded in making them a star—like Nancy, Kristi, Katarina, and Oksana—there are probably hundreds of other women who aspired to be great skaters and who made similar sacrifices, without ever making it to the top. Nancy Kerrigan was one of the lucky ones whose persistence paid off.

The summer before her freshman year at Stoneham High School, 14-year-old Nancy and her mother went to the principal's office to ask for a special schedule. Nancy wanted all of her classes to be in the morning, so she could spend each afternoon at the practice rink. The principal was surprised that someone so young could be that dedicated to one activity. He suggested that Nancy take an extra course or

USFSA judges were impressed with Nancy's elegant skating.

This illustration shows how skaters use the front and back inside and outside edges of their skate blades to trace compulsory or "school" figures on the ice. In the 1960s, compulsory figures counted for a major part of a skater's overall score, but in 1990, the USFSA eliminated school figures from competition.

two, in case she wanted to change her mind someday and do something other than ice skate. But Nancy knew even then that she would rather spend every moment she could in the skating rink.

Nancy was not a very outgoing student in high school. Like her days in elementary school, she spent so many hours training that she didn't have the time or the energy to socialize with her classmates. There were days when she would come home very upset, because she didn't feel like she had any friends. But even though Nancy was never the most popular girl in her high school, her classmates respected her ambition, and thought that one day she would be famous and successful. When Nancy graduated from Stoneham High School, in 1987, the yearbook listed her as the person most likely to win an Olympic medal.

Every skating competition has two parts. The first part is a two-and-one-half minute routine known as the short program which includes several compulsory moves, including three jumps, three spins, and two sequences of footwork. The jumps and spins that skaters do during their programs vary in difficulty. In general, the more difficult a move, the more credit a skater will get for doing it successfully. This is particularly true of the jumps: the flip, the Salchow, the toe loop, the Lutz, and the Axel. Of these, the most difficult is the Axel. A jump can be a single, a double, or a triple, depending on how many revolutions the skater turns once he or she is up in the air. Most women who skate competitively can turn triple (three revolutions in the air) flips, toe loops Lutzes, and Salchows. The Axel is usually doubled (two revolutions in the air) by women skaters, although a few female skaters can land triple Axels.

The second part of the skating competition, the long or freestyle program, is four minutes long. Skating for four minutes, and making many jumps and spins, is very tiring. For skaters, four minutes can last forever. The short program counts for one-third of a skater's final score, and the long program counts for the remaining two-thirds. This method of scoring was introduced by the United States Figure Skating Association (USFSA) in 1990. Prior to that time, skaters had to compete in an additional competition, known as the compulsory figures. Compulsory figures are shapes that skaters have to be able to trace on the ice with their skate blades, using different blade edges.

Nancy's first major medal in competition was the bronze she won at the 1991 Worlds held in Munich, Germany. American women dominated the competition, with Kristi Yamaguchi (center) earning the gold medal, and Tonya Harding (left) winning the silver.

Beginning from a standstill, the skater is allowed only so many push-offs for each figure and must be able to complete the tracing accurately and carefully before running out of momentum. In addition, a skater must use the specified edge—either the inside or outside front or back edge—to create the figure. Skaters are judged on the accuracy of their tracing as well as their posture and their ability to maintain a steady, smooth speed. There are 42 different compulsory figures, and though a skater might only be asked to perform a few in competition, there was no way of knowing which figures would be selected by the judges. Earlier in the twentieth century, the figures counted for a large portion of a skater's overall score in competition, but by the time of their elimination they counted for only one-third of a skater's score. This is because skating was emphasizing artistry and choreography more than at any other time in its history. And unlike the short and long programs, which showcased a skater's artistry and athleticism, the compulsories were an unexciting aspect of competition. Skating events were beginning to enjoy increased television viewership; they were appealing to a broad audience, and that audience was bored by the compulsory figures.

Since compulsories are the building blocks for many skating moves, skaters still learn the compulsories as part of their training, but most are happy not to be scored on them in competition.

The skaters' routines are marked by seven judges who rate the competitors on technical merit and artistic impression. Technical merit is based on whether the jumps are landed correctly on one foot, without faltering or falling, and whether the spins are completed. Artistic merit covers the elegance, grace, and artistry that a skater gives to her performance. It's not enough for a skater to land jumps and perform spins without falling down. Skating requires a certain amount of style and finesse. In this way, it is different from many other sports, such as basketball, tennis, or track and field events. In those sports, whoever scores the most points, or runs a given distance in the fastest time is the clear winner. In skating, more personal judgment goes into determining who wins a competition.

By the time she graduated from high school, Nancy had already skated well at four major competitions. In 1985 she placed second at the Eastern Junior Sectionals. That year she skated at the U.S. National Juniors competition for the first time and placed 11th. The following year Nancy took fourth place at the Eastern Junior Regionals, second at the New England Junior

Regionals, and 11th again at the U.S. National Juniors. By 1987 she had improved enough to place fourth at the National Juniors.

After graduating from Stoneham High in 1987, Nancy was able to devote more time to skating. She spent that summer in intensive training, while working as a waitress to help pay her expenses. After so many years of watching her father work extra jobs to pay for her training, Nancy was happy to be able to help pay her own way.

In the fall of 1987 Nancy chose to remain close to home and enrolled in Emmanuel College, a women's college in Boston. The following winter she won her most impressive tournament to date, taking top honors in the National Collegiate Championships. In 1989 Nancy competed for the first time in the U.S. Nationals Championship, the competition that determines which skaters will represent America on the Olympic team.

When the competition began, no one in the skating world really knew about Nancy Kerrigan, except that she was a collegiate skating champion. But Nancy surprised the judges, who were impressed with her elegant skating and tasteful outfits. She placed fifth. She finished one rung higher in each of the next four years, finally gaining the championship in 1993.

Her third place finish in the 1991 Nationals gave Nancy the opportunity to skate in her first World Championships in April of that year. Nancy was honored to be competing in this event, where the best skaters in the world gathered each year. Few people thought she had a chance to be among the top ten. They considered her third place finish in the 1991 Nationals a fluke because Jill Trenary, who had won the Nationals the year before, was injured and unable to compete. Had Trenary skated, some people projected, Nancy would not have finished in the top three, and she would not have been invited to skate in the World Championships.

But Nancy had skated in the Nationals, and her performance showed that she belonged there. Her short program was crisp and elegant, and gave her high enough scores to put her in fifth place going into the long program. Although her performance in the short program may have surprised some people, those closest to Nancy were not shocked. Nancy had always skated well in the short programs. Her weakness was usually the more demanding long program.

At the 1991 World Championships, though, Nancy rose to the occasion, surprising even herself with her terrific free skate. Her performance in the long program gave her a third place finish. Out of nowhere, Nancy Kerrigan had won the bronze at the World Championships. It was Nancy's first major medal in an international competition, but it would not be her last. In less than a year, she would be skating at the one competition that was more important than the Worlds—the 1992 Winter Olympics.

A Tale of
Two Skaters

After the 1992 Olympics, Nancy's life changed. Suddenly, she was an Olympic medal winner, and she was famous. People recognized her on the street. They asked for her autograph, and they wanted her picture. Soon after Albertville, Nancy's friend Kristi Yamaguchi announced that she was going to turn professional, which meant that she could receive money for skating. According to Olympic rules at that time, a skater who was paid for skating was not allowed to compete in the Olympics.

Kristi Yamaguchi's retirement from amateur skating meant that Nancy was suddenly one of two young women who were competing to be the top skater in the United States. The other skater was Tonya Harding, who had won

With Kristi Yamaguchi turning pro, Tonya Harding became Nancy Kerrigan's major American competitor.

the U.S. Nationals in 1991, and who had also skated at the 1991 Worlds and the 1992 Olympic games along with Nancy and Kristi.

One month after the Olympic games, Nancy placed second at the 1992 World Championships. Then, in January of 1993, Nancy won the United States National championships.

The year 1993 was an unusual one. It was only one year after the 1992 Olympics, but it was also only one year before the next Olympics. The Winter Olympics had formerly taken place every four years, along with the summer games. Olympic officials decided to separate the games, so that every two years one type of Olympics would be held. The start of this schedule meant that the next winter Games would occur in 1994.

This meant that Nancy had only two years to prepare for the Olympics, rather than the four that skaters had always had in the past. This also meant that the winner of the 1993 championships was immediately seen as the American favorite at the 1994 games. When Nancy won the Nationals in 1993, she began to get a lot of attention. She was named one of the 50 most beautiful women by *People* magazine, and she was interviewed often by members of the media. Photographers trailed her.

Nancy was not used to that much attention, and it interfered with her concentration. In the spring of 1993, she went to the World Championships in Prague favored to win a medal. But Nancy did not skate a good long program. She missed her first jump and turned two triple jumps into singles. Despite having won first place in the short program, Nancy ended up a disappointing fifth. The 1993 Worlds at Prague was one of the lowest points in Nancy's skating career.

After the World Championships, Nancy decided she would need to work extra hard if she wanted to go to the Olympics and win a medal. So she began training extra hours, sometimes skating her long programs twice or even three times in a row without stopping.

"In some ways," she said, "What happened in Prague might have been the best thing for me. I was very mad at myself. It made me fight harder." By the time of the 1994 Nationals, Nancy felt strong and confident that she could win the title once again and be named as one of the members of the 1994 Olympic figure skating team. She knew the competition would be tough. In addition to Tonya Harding, a 13-year-old skater named Michelle Kwan was also skating at the Nationals.

The Nationals were held at the Joe Louis Arena in Detroit. Nancy knew she would have to

A distraught Dan and Brenda Kerrigan listen to Dr. Mahlon Bradley explain their daughter Nancy's condition at a press conference following her attack at the 1994 Nationals in Detroit. Nancy, whose knee and thigh were badly bruised and swollen after being struck with a lead pipe, was forced to withdraw from the competition.

skate her best there in order to beat the competition and win the Nationals.

On January 6, Nancy was walking in the arena with her father when a man came out of the shadows and hit her on the leg with a lead pipe. Before Nancy knew it, she was on the floor, screaming in shock and pain. Her father lifted Nancy in his arms and carried her to a hospital.

Nancy had no broken bones, but her knee and parts of her thigh were badly swollen and bruised. She would not be able to skate in the competition. Usually the top two finishers at the National Championships would be on the Olympic figure skating team. Since she was too injured to skate, there seemed to be no way that she would be allowed to skate in the Olympics. But, considering that she had been unfairly eliminated from a competition she was expected to win, United States Olympic Committee (USOC) officials invited her to skate on the team. In the meantime, Tonya Harding won the Nationals, and Michelle Kwan finished in second place. Nancy Kerrigan and Tonya Harding would be the two women skaters on the United States Olympic team.

A few days after the 1994 Nationals ended, police charged a man named Shane Stant with assaulting Nancy with the lead pipe. Then authorities learned that Stant had been hired by a man named Sean Eckardt, who lived in Portland, Oregon, Tonya Harding's hometown.

Detectives probed further and learned that Eckardt was a friend of Jeff Gilooly, Tonya Harding's former husband. Gilooly was brought in by the FBI, who asked him if he knew anything about how and why Nancy Kerrigan had been attacked. Gilooly admitted that he had hired Eckardt to hurt Nancy and put her out of the Nationals. Gilooly went on to say that Eckardt had asked Stant to do the job of actually injuring Nancy with the lead pipe, and that Stant and Eckardt had been trying for several weeks to find Nancy and to hurt her.

Then Gilooly told the FBI something very surprising. He said that Tonya Harding knew about these plans, and that she had even helped the three men by telling them where Nancy would be, and when would be a good time to attack her.

The nation was shocked when this news was reported. One figure skater had purposely planned a vicious attack on another skater, in order to win an important competition. When detectives asked Tonya Harding what she knew about the situation, though, she said that she didn't know anything about it. She told them

The press followed Nancy everywhere after her attack at the 1994 Nationals, hoping for comments on the alleged plot to assault her. The publicity upset Kerrigan, shown here being escorted by her agent Jerry Solomon.

she had learned about the attack only after it had happened; she didn't know why Nancy had been injured, but she thought that maybe Jeff Gilooly was very anxious for her to win the competition and to skate for the Olympic team.

But Gilooly said that Tonya Harding was lying—she did know about it, and she had helped plan it. This was a very serious accusation. If Tonya Harding did take part in the plot to injure Nancy, as Gilooly said she did, then she would not be allowed to skate in the Olympic Games.

Nancy's injury slowly healed. Through intensive physical therapy, she was able to walk, then to run, and finally, to skate, without pain. But she had lost valuable time; the Olympics were less than six weeks away, and Nancy would have to be in tip-top shape in order to hope for a medal. She began doing special exercises in order to get stronger, including swimming, lifting weights, and biking. She knew that she would have to be relaxed as well as fit in order to skate well, so she spent a lot of time listening to comedy tapes to make her laugh.

Nancy was lucky that she had a close family to help her with some of her final preparations for the Lillehammer games. Despite her blindness, her mother ironed the skating costumes with the help of Nancy's father, who guided her hand. The dining room of the Kerrigans' Massachusetts home had several tubs that were overflowing with mail from people who were rooting for her.

The extra training and exercises had helped her get her strength back, and her leg was almost completely healed. But one thing Nancy had not been able to do during this time was to skate in front of a live audience. Her coach believed that Nancy would have to have this

Skating before a live audience for the first time since her attack a month earlier at the Nationals, Nancy hams it up at "Nancy Kerrigan and Friends," a special ice show held in her honor in February of 1994.

experience before skating in the Olympics. So a special event, called "Nancy Kerrigan and Friends," was arranged.

On February 5, 1994, one month after she had been attacked, Nancy Kerrigan took the ice to skate a difficult program in front of a large audience in Boston. Nancy's friends and family came out to cheer her on. She skated well, landing all of her jumps. She also looked relaxed and confident. Her coach felt that her spins needed more speed, but everyone was happy about the amazing progress Nancy had made. After skating in Boston, she was ready to go to Norway and to the Olympics.

On February 15, eight days before the start of the Olympic figure skating competition, the United States Olympic Committee (USOC) called Tonya Harding to a special hearing. They demanded that Harding answer Gilooly's charges that she knew about and had participated in his plan to injure Nancy Kerrigan. Tonya Harding refused to appear, threatening to sue the USOC for $25 million for making this

After her attack at the 1994 Nationals, Nancy had to regain her confidence by practicing in front of live audiences.

demand. The USOC said it would cancel the hearing if Harding would cancel her lawsuit. Because nothing could be done to prove that Tonya Harding had participated in the plot, the USOC gave Harding the go-ahead to skate in the Olympics.

For Nancy, this would mean that she would be on an Olympic team with a person whom many believed had tried to hurt her. In addition, the drama surrounding Nancy Kerrigan and Tonya Harding had made international head-lines. People all over the world now knew what had taken place that January night in Detroit. These fans would most certainly be watching the skating competition to find out how the story would end. Like it or not, Nancy Kerrigan and Tonya Harding would be the center of the world's attention at the 1994 Olympic games.

For Nancy Kerrigan the 1994 Olympics at Lillehammer would be different from the games at Albertville two years earlier. At Albertville she had not been in the limelight, and had not been expected to win. Now she was the top skater in the United States, and expectations for her were high. In addition, the situation between her and Tonya Harding had become a fascinating drama, not only for Americans, but for the entire world. A record audience tuned in to watch the Olympics in 1994, and one of the reasons for that large following was the saga involving Nancy and Tonya.

The hardest two weeks of Nancy's life were about to begin.

TRIUMPH AT LILLEHAMMER

At the 1994 winter Olympics, cameras followed both Nancy and Tonya during the practice routines. On the first day of practice for them, more than 700 members of the media waited at the rink, anticipating what the meeting of the two skaters would be like. Nancy was already on the ice practicing when Tonya Harding arrived about ten minutes later.

As Tonya skated onto the ice, Nancy gave her a "special welcome," as the press called it, by turning a triple Lutz–double toe combination that she landed close to the other skater. Tonya pretended not to notice. That was about as close as the two skaters came to acknowledging one another's presence. On the whole, Tonya Harding and Nancy Kerrigan spent a

---

Nancy Kerrigan practices before a crowd ten times larger than normal at the Hamar Olympic Amphitheatre in 1994.

little more than an hour practicing together that day, and there were no collisions or harsh words, nor was there any contact at all between them.

Nancy Kerrigan looked much more in shape and ready for the competition during the practice sessions than Tonya Harding did. Nancy was skating with grace and confidence, flying through both her short and long programs fairly easily. Harding was suffering from a sore ankle. She was also constantly short of breath. Although she suffered from asthma, Tonya had a fairly heavy smoking habit. That also may have interfered with her skating during those practice sessions. She fell often, and frequently turned her triple jumps into single ones. She seemed to lack the energy and the drive that she would need to do well in the Olympics.

Despite her flashy welcome for Tonya, Nancy didn't like the intense media attention the controversy had thrust upon her. It seemed as though every time she brushed her teeth, there was a member of the press there with a camera or a notebook. She also missed her friends from the 1992 games, where she had roomed with Kristi Yamaguchi and spent a great deal of time with Paul Wylie. In Lillehammer she didn't spend much time with her teammates. Nancy stayed in a private residence with her family far from the Olympic village.

Nancy was not in Lillehammer for the entire games. She came to Norway about a week before the ladies' competition was to begin, during the last few days of the schedule. For women skaters, the wait to begin skating has always been a long one. In 1994, with the eyes of the world on Nancy Kerrigan and Tonya Harding, the time in Lillehammer before the competition was to begin seemed endless.

In addition to her rivalry with Tonya Harding, Nancy had other things on her mind. She had not skated well at her last international skating event, the 1993 World Championships in Prague. She had performed poorly in her long program and finished fifth. She knew that she tended to skate well during her short program, as she had in Albertville, but that her long programs were always slightly shakier. She would have to skate perfectly during both programs in order to win an Olympic medal against a strong field.

Despite the intense pressure of the previous weeks and the media hype surrounding her attack and Tonya Harding's presence on the U.S. team, Nancy Kerrigan, shown leaning back during a spin in her short program, was able to concentrate on her skating and placed first in the technical program.

Many people thought the French skater Surya Bonaly, who had finished fourth at the Albertville games, would win the gold. A skater from China named Chen Lu was a favorite with fans and judges. Although small and very thin, Ukrainian Oksana Baiul had become a very strong skater with a distinctive balletic style. Many experts thought she would be the top choice for gold.

And there was Tonya Harding. Although she was a controversial choice and many people thought she should not even be skating in Lillehammer, Tonya Harding was a strong athletic skater. She was the only female skater in the 1994 games who had ever landed a triple Axel in competition. A two-time national champion, Harding had told the press that the only thing she ever wanted was an Olympic gold medal, and that she was not going to stop until she got one. Like it or not, Nancy had to take her seriously.

At long last the short program began, and almost everyone skated beautifully. Surya Bonaly skated an athletic program and scored high marks. Oksana Baiul's routine was more like a ballet; she landed one of her combinations on two skates instead of one, which cost her some points. China's Chen Lu also skated well.

Tonya Harding did not skate her best during the short program. She landed all her jumps, but several times she came down on both skates instead of one. And on her opening move, which was supposed to be a triple Lutz–double toe loop combination, she took a step between the two jumps. This meant that she would not receive credit for a combination, which was one of the required elements. She also seemed slightly off in her timing, unable to skate in step with her music. It looked after the short program as though Tonya Harding would not win an Olympic medal. Perhaps the pressure of the publicity leading up to the Olympics had made a difference to Harding.

It did not seem to have affected Kerrigan, whose short program was close to perfect. The moment Nancy skated onto the ice in her white skating dress with sheer black sleeves, her confidence and appealing smile showed the crowd that she was, at least for the time being, able to forget the intensity of the previous seven weeks and skate her heart out. Pausing while the sellout crowd of 6,000 calmed down after having wildly cheered her arrival, Kerrigan then glided smoothly into her first element, which was the required combination of two jumps. Nancy had planned to perform her triple Lutz–double toe loop combination—a move that could make or break her performance. Building momentum, she launched into the air, rotated three times cleanly and elegantly through the triple Lutz, landed smoothly, and then pulled off a double toe loop immediately. When Nancy spun twice and landed the double toe loop perfectly on one blade, the crowd erupted into enthusiastic cheers. Her coach Evy Scotvold, sitting just a few feet away at the rail, threw his hands into the air with excitement. What both Scotvold and Kerrigan knew was that the hardest part of her routine was now over. And Nancy, smile flashing, went on to nail a high flying double Axel, then a double flip with ease. Overall, Nancy's short program was thrilling. Other than some minor errors in her footwork late in the program, she had skated a perfect program. The judges awarded her two 5.6s, four 5.8s, and three 5.9s (out of a perfect score of 6.0) for technical performance. Her artistic marks were also impressive: one 5.6, two 5.7s, two 5.8s, and one 5.9. Overall, Nancy was rated first by seven of the nine skating judges.

Nancy was followed in the standings by Oksana Baiul in second place. Despite her technical mistake, Oksana had impressed the judges with her balletic artistry, receiving six 5.9s for artistic merit from the judges. Surya Bonaly was third and China's Chen Lu fourth after the short program. Tonya Harding was in tenth place going into the long program. This meant that she would be skating before the top medal contenders.

Relieved and happy at the end of the short program, Nancy told the huge group of reporters that she was very proud of herself. "I guess I've dreamed about it," she said, "but it's more than day-dreaming. It's hard work. Dreams won't get you there." Her coach, Mary Scotvold, was enthusiastic. "I'm just so emotionally moved by it," Scotvold told reporters. "She was so deliberate in everything she did, every gesture, every jump. It was just very exciting to see her do that after these seven weeks."

On the morning of the long program, something happened on the ice that turned many people's heads. While practicing her routine, Oksana Baiul collided with a German skater named Tanja Szewczenko. Both girls landed hard on the ice. Oksana Baiul was bruised and cut and very upset. The people who had seen the accident thought that Oksana Baiul might be too injured to skate well that night. The competition, already the object of fascination around the world, became even more dramatic.

For the long program, the skaters are divided into groups of six depending on how well they place during the short program. The groups then skate in reverse order, so that the top six skaters skate last. Since Tonya Harding was tenth after the short program, she would skate in the third group of six skaters. Kerrigan, first after the short program, skated in the fourth and final group.

Tonya Harding was to be the sixth and final skater in her group. But long after the fifth skater had left the ice and received her scores, Harding was nowhere in sight. The public address system announced her name as the next competitor. For several minutes no one appeared.

Finally Tonya emerged from the locker room, hurried onto the ice and skated to the center. But from the moment she began her long program, it was clear that something was wrong. She was having a hard time jumping, and she could barely keep her balance during her spins. Finally, Tonya Harding stopped skating. Pointing to her feet, she skated to the sidelines where the judges were seated. She put one of her skates on the railing for the head judge to see, and explained that her lace had broken and she had not had the time to change it.

No skater had ever stopped in the middle of a routine and asked for the chance to skate again. But the Lillehammer games were clearly an exception to all Olympics. The judge told Harding she could start again.

She began her long program for the second time, and was able to get through it without a major fall. She hit four triple jumps, although she never tried the triple Axel, which she had landed during previous competitions. At the end of the program, she took a bow and left the ice. She would finish eighth.

The Olympics were over for Tonya Harding, but for Nancy Kerrigan, there was still a long program to skate. Nancy was skating second to last among the women in medal contention. The first to skate, Surya Bonaly, did not perform well during the long program. An athletic skater, Bonaly was not as graceful or elegant on the ice as many skaters who win Olympic medals. This weakness showed during her long program, and because she did not skate as cleanly as she could have, Bonaly received low marks. Chen Lu, however, skated a beautiful long program. Though not as athletic as Surya Bonaly's, it was clean and elegant. The judges liked what they saw and gave Chen Lu good marks.

Then it was Nancy Kerrigan's turn. She skated slowly to the center of the ice. It could very well be that at that moment before the long program, as she stood there, waiting for her music to begin, she remembered the long training hours in Stoneham, Massachusetts, and the early competitions. She might have remembered the early morning and late night practices, and the sacrifices her family cheerfully made for her to make it this far. She might also have been thinking about the events of the past two months—how she had been attacked in a rink in Detroit and injured with only weeks to go before the Olympics.

Whatever she was thinking during those moments, Nancy Kerrigan would have to put it out of her mind once she began to skate to her music, a medley of Neil Diamond tunes. Her first jump was supposed to be a triple, and she turned it into a double. But after that rather slow beginning, Nancy began to gather momentum. She landed jump after jump, including five triples—most of them in combination—and a double Axel. Nancy twirled elegantly, and, it seemed, endlessly. Her smile, hesitant at the beginning of the long program, became broader as her routine progressed. At the end, Nancy spun around in the center of the ice. She finished with a flourish, arms held high above her head. Her long program was behind her, and Nancy had triumphed. With the eyes of the world upon her, she skated superbly.

After leaving the ice, Nancy hugged her coaches and laughed in sheer delight and relief. The demons of Prague were over. She had, at long last, skated a truly magnificent long program.

Nancy's scores for technical merit and artistic impression were high. Many observers felt sure that Nancy had won the gold after watching her performance and seeing her scores. Then Oksana Baiul, the last of the 24 women to compete, took the ice. Everyone knew there was a possibility that she could beat Nancy, but it would take a flawless routine in order for that

In an unprecedented move, Tonya Harding stopped skating during her performance at the 1994 Olympics and showed her skate to the judges, telling them her lace had broken. The judges allowed her to fix her skate and begin again. Harding was out of the running after the freestyle program and finished eighth.

Olympic medalists Nancy Kerrigan, Oksana Baiul, and Chen Lu wave to the crowd after receiving their medals. Nancy, who won the silver medal, was beaten out for the gold by Ukrainian Oksana Baiul (center) who scored just one tenth of one point higher than her. Chen Lu, of China, took third place.

to happen. Oksana Baiul was still shaken from the collision with the German skater earlier that day, and no one knew if she would be able to skate well. In addition, many people believed that Oksana Baiul, who was not as athletic a skater as Nancy Kerrigan, did not have a long program that was difficult enough technically to compete with Nancy's stunning performance. All in all, if Oksana Baiul had any hope of grabbing the gold medal from Nancy Kerrigan that night, she would have to skate masterfully.

Oksana Baiul would be skating to a routine that featured music from several Broadway musicals. After landing a triple Lutz masterfully,

Baiul stumbled for a minute, and landed one of her jumps on two skates instead of one. To make up for that mistake, Baiul threw in an extra jump—a triple Salchow, which she landed perfectly. As the program continued, Oksana Baiul gathered confidence, and her artistry was truly a thing of beauty. At the end of her routine, with what might be the gold medal at stake, Oksana Baiul added yet another jump—a triple toe loop—that she had not been scheduled to do. Then she landed a double Axel-double toe combination at the end of her routine, and burst into tears of relief.

In the end, the scoring between Kerrigan and Baiul came down to a fraction of a point. The judges rated Baiul's long program slightly above Kerrigan's. Five judges rated Baiul first, and four rated Kerrigan first, giving Oksana the gold and Nancy the silver. Chen Lu secured the bronze.

Nancy Kerrigan did not win the gold, but she had put on the performance of her career. It may have been the one time in Olympic history when the color of the medal did not really seem to matter. What counted for the millions of fans around the world was the triumph of the human spirit—that one person could come back from a violent attack to skate in the most pressured of competitions and win a medal. For that, Nancy Kerrigan would always be remembered and celebrated.

"She might not have gotten the gold, but she did too many things much bigger than the gold," one of her coaches, Evy Scotvold, said of Nancy's performance during the games, "and I hope she never loses sight of that because what she faced and overcame is much bigger than a gold medal."

ELEGANCE ON ICE

Nancy was both relieved and disappointed when the 1994 Olympic games ended. She was disappointed because she had come so close to winning a gold medal, but it had eluded her. She was relieved and happy, though, that she had skated so well. For that reason, she would always think of Lillehammer as a victory.

Hoping to put much of the media hype behind her, Nancy decided that she would retire from amateur competition and become a professional skater. She realized that she had spent a great deal of her life practicing skating, and now she wanted to do other things.

Kerrigan returned from Lillehammer a hero. Victory parades were held in her honor in her hometown of Stoneham, Massachusetts, and she made public appearances in places

Nancy Kerrigan waves to the crowd during a parade held in her honor at Disney World.

like Disney World. She also tried her hand at comedy, appearing as host of the television program *Saturday Night Live*. Then in November Nancy made her debut as a professional skater, performing in an exhibition called "Ice Wars" with fellow Olympic medalists Kristi Yamaguchi and Oksana Baiul.

The first few months after Lillehammer were not always easy ones for Nancy. One of the hardest things she had to face was that, although the Olympics had ended, she was still at the center of public attention. Interest in skating usually died down after an Olympics, but this year was different. The Harding/Kerrigan rivalry had helped transform figure skating's image. Suddenly everyone was interested in women's and men's figure skating, pairs skating, and ice dancing. Television executives

Nancy Kerrigan smiles at her husband and agent, Jerry Solomon, following their wedding at the Church of the Covenant in Boston, September 9, 1995.

began promoting skating events, and ABC signed a 10-year, 100-million-dollar contract with the USFSA. Only pro-football games garner more viewers than figure skating now. Millions of Americans watch skating specials. The public continued to be interested in Nancy Kerrigan after the 1994 winter Olympics, and Nancy had not been prepared for that. There were times when Nancy seemed tense and not at ease when talking to the press or in public. Some people thought that she did not seem gracious on the victory stand when Oksana Baiul was awarded her gold medal. At the Disney World parade, some people overheard her tell her mother that the parade was "the corniest thing I've ever seen."

But Nancy was not trying to be unkind or ungracious. As she explained to the press, she was not used to being in the public eye for such a long period of time. In the words of fellow Olympic skater Scott Hamilton, Nancy had been living "under an electron microscope," ever since the 1994 Nationals. The media and the public's fixation with her had been stressful to Nancy, and she was uncomfortable with having to live her life in public. Like everyone else, she had made some mistakes. Most Americans understood that, and they understood Nancy's desire for privacy.

Tonya Harding returned to America after the Olympics and pleaded guilty to knowing about the conspiracy to injure Nancy Kerrigan. She was fined, had her two National championships taken away from her, and was banned from skating in competitions. Harding returned to the Portland, Oregon, area where she started a band and worked as an actress.

In February 1998, before the start of the Olympic games in Nagano, Japan, Nancy

Four months after giving birth to son Matthew, Nancy was back on the ice, performing at the 1997 U.S. Professional Figure Skating Championships held in San Jose, California.

Kerrigan and Tonya Harding appeared on "Breaking the Ice" a television special where they talked together about their memories of what had happened four years earlier. Nancy had agreed to the interview, despite her distaste for the intense media coverage following her attack in 1994, because, as she put it, "[I] knew that someone was going to bring it up, and I figured in a controlled setting, it would be a lot safer and more comfortable to be involved." The media frenzy that surrounded Kerrigan and

Harding up until the 1994 Olympics became the subject of a 1996 book called *Women on Ice: Feminist Responses to the Tonya Harding/Nancy Kerrigan Spectacle.* The book questioned the public's obsession with the two skaters and examined the ways the media portrayed the women as well as the roles figure skaters are expected to fulfill. Harding apologized to Nancy for the difficulty she went through after she had been injured.

During the 1998 Olympics, Kerrigan began hosting figure skating events for "Front Row," a sports program on New England Cable News.

In September 1995 Nancy married her agent, Jerry Solomon. They moved into a house in Lynnfield, Massachusetts, about eight miles away from where Nancy's family lives. Nancy had a little boy named Matthew in December, 1996. Though Nancy was excited to be a new mother, she also planned to continue skating, and she had to work hard to regain her fitness level. After gaining 23 pounds during her pregnancy, Nancy needed to return to her prepregnancy weight. Seven weeks after Matthew's birth, she began exercising in a swimming pool, strengthening her muscle groups by doing abdominal crunches with a floating barbell. With the help of Igor Burdenko, a sports-medicine consultant and founder of the Burdenko Water and Sports Therapy Institute in Lexington, Massachusetts, Nancy got back into shape. In February she resumed training with the Scotvolds, practicing her triple jumps and a new three and a half minute routine for her exhibition tour. Four months after she gave birth, Nancy was on the ice performing again in professional competitions and exhibitions.

"Now she's skating for herself," said Nancy's long-time coach, Evy Scotvold. "She still has that competitive [spirit], because she's a competitor, but now she laughs more. She'll look over at Matthew and she'll smile and laugh; she's much more relaxed."

In October of 1997 Nancy competed in the U.S. Pro Figure Skating Championships, the first of five events leading to the World Professional Championships at the end of the year. In her short program, to the theme of "The Indian in the Cupboard," Nancy landed two triple toe loops and one double Axel, but turned a planned triple Salchow into a single. She received high marks for both her short and long programs, and though she competed against other skating giants like Kristi Yamaguchi, Katarina Witt, and Ekaterina Gordeeva, Kerrigan came in third.

Not wanting to miss a day with her son, Nancy took him with her on the 1998 Campbell Soup Champions on Ice tour, along with her mother, who loved to babysit.

Today Nancy skates for the fun of it. She participates in some professional competitions, but for the most part she skates in exhibitions. She also hosts a television program on ice skating that is shown in Massachusetts.

Nancy has appeared in numerous advertisements for companies like Campbell Soup, Walt Disney World, Ray Ban, J.C. Penny, Seiko, and Reebok. She has also worked with the Spaulding Rehabilitation Hospital in Boston to develop the "Nancy Kerrigan Performance Program," an educational program that helps athletes and others to improve their performance level. In addition, she has donated her time to help charities like the Massachusetts Children's Trust Fund, which helps abused children. Nancy has also been the spokesperson for the Lion's Club's SightFirst Campaign, an initiative which seeks to eradicate preventable and reversible blindness around the world by providing people with proper medical attention and treatment.

Enjoying a private life for the first time since her attack in 1994, Nancy Kerrigan is now able to enjoy her family and her career without the pressure of succeeding in front of millions of people. With her style and grace on the skating rink as evident now as it has always been, Nancy Kerrigan remains a symbol of elegance on ice.

CHRONOLOGY

1968 Born in Stoneham, Massachusetts, on February 7.

1985 Finishes second in first junior figure skating championship, the Eastern Junior Sectionals.

1988 Wins National Collegiate Championship.

1989 Places fifth at Nationals.

1991 Places third at Nationals and third at Worlds.

1992 Finishes second at Nationals and places second at Worlds; wins bronze medal at Olympic Games in Albertville.

1993 Wins Nationals and places fifth at Worlds.

1994 Attacked with lead pipe at 1994 United States Nationals; wins silver medal at Olympic Games in Lillehammer; turns professional.

1995 Marries Jerry Solomon.

1996 Gives birth to Matthew Solomon.

FURTHER READING

Nelson, Rebecca and Marie J. Macnee, eds. *The Olympic Handbook.* Detroit: Visible Inc., 1996.

Ryan, Joan. *Little Girls in Pretty Boxes: The Making and Breaking of Elite Gymnasts and Figure Skaters.* New York: Doubleday, 1995.

Wallechinsky, David. *SI Presents The Complete Book of the Olympics.* Boston: Little Brown, 1996.

ABOUT THE AUTHOR

Paula Edelson is a freelance writer and journalist. She lives with her husband and two sons in Durham, North Carolina, and is the author of the Chelsea House books *Superstars of Men's Tennis* and *Superstars of Men's Swimming and Diving.*

GLOSSARY

AXEL: a jump named for its inventor, Axel Paulsen. The Axel is the only jump launched while skating forward. A skater takes off from the forward outside skate edge and lands on the opposite foot on a back outside edge. A double Axel is the same jump with two and a half mid-air rotations. A triple Axel, achieved for the first time in 1978, requires three and a half mid-air rotations.

CAMEL: a skating spin performed with one leg extended back; the camel is called a flying camel when a skater jumps into the spin.

CROSSOVER: performed when a skater crosses his or her stride; a crossover tends to increase a skater's speed.

DEATH SPIRAL: a pairs figure skating move in which the man pivots and spins the woman in a circle around him with one hand while her arched body spirals down until it is almost parallel to the ice.

FLIP: a jump made by sticking the blade pick into the ice, revolving, and then landing on the back outside edge of the toe-assisting foot; the triple flip is the same jump with three revolutions.

FOOTWORK: any series of turns, steps, hops, and crossovers done at high speed.

LIFTS: pairs moves in which the man holds the woman up in a ballet-like position over his head; variations on lifts include the star lift, in which the woman holds both her arms in the air, and the one-armed lift, in which the man supports the woman with only one arm.

LOOP: a jump in which the skater takes off and lands on the same back outside edge.

LUTZ: a jump named for its creator, Alois Lutz. For the Lutz, a skater takes off on a back outside edge, revolves, and then lands on a back outside edge. When a skater revolves three times in the air, the jump is called a triple Lutz.

SALCHOW: a jump named after Swedish skater Ulrich Salchow. For the Salchow, a skater makes a long glide backward and then takes off on the outside edge of one skate, with a boost from the toe of the opposite skate. After revolving, the skater lands on the outside edge of the boosting skate. A double Salchow has two rotations; a triple Salchow requires three full rotations while in the air.

SPIN: a skater performs a spin by rotating from one fixed point; when skaters spin, they move so fast their image becomes blurred.

SIT SPIN: a spin in which the skater crouches down, balanced on one leg while the other extends; often a skater will pull up out of a sit spin to a standing spin position.

SPREAD-EAGLE: a move in which a skater glides on two feet, with the lead foot on a forward edge and the trail foot on the same edge, only backward.

TOE LOOP: a jump launched off the toe pick of the free foot in which a skater completes one rotation and lands on the back outside edge of the same foot. The toe pick can launch the skater to a great height; hence, a double toe loop has two mid-air rotations, and a triple toe loop has three.

THROWS: pairs moves in which the man throws the woman into the air, where she spins two or three times before landing on one foot.

INDEX

Picture Credits: AP/Wide World Photos: pp. 2, 6, 9, 16, 23, 26, 30, 33, 35, 37, 38, 40, 43, 49, 50, 52, 54, 56, 60; New York Public Library: pp. 12, 18, 21, 24